Baby Jesus
Like My Brother

by Margery Wheeler Brown   Illustrations by George Ford

For Cory
—M.W.B.

For Wade and Cheryl Hudson
who, with dedication and wisdom,
perform miracles every day.

I love you both.

—G.F.

Baby Jesus
Like My Brother

by Margery Wheeler Brown   Illustrations by George Ford

Printed in China   First Edition   10 9 8 7 6 5 4 3 2 1
Library of Congress Catalog Number 95-76530
ISBN: 0-940975-53-X Hardcover edition 0-940975-54-8 Paperback edition

JUST US BOOKS

East Orange, New Jersey

1995

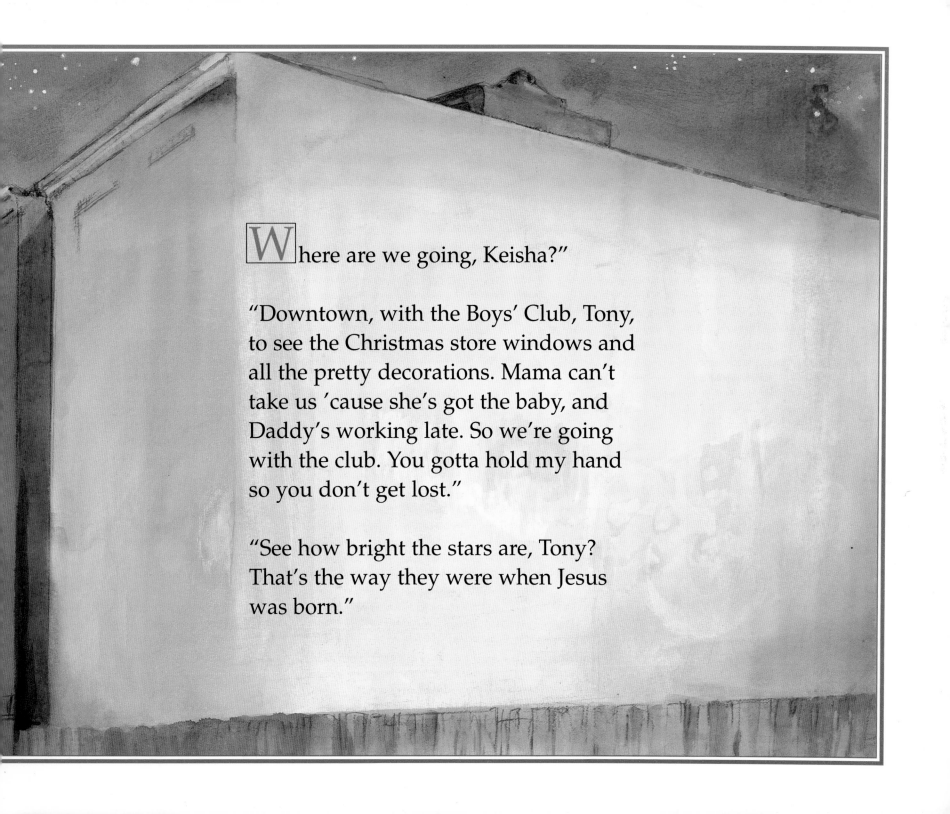

"Where are we going, Keisha?"

"Downtown, with the Boys' Club, Tony, to see the Christmas store windows and all the pretty decorations. Mama can't take us 'cause she's got the baby, and Daddy's working late. So we're going with the club. You gotta hold my hand so you don't get lost."

"See how bright the stars are, Tony? That's the way they were when Jesus was born."

"Tell me 'bout Jesus, Keisha."

"He was a good man who lived
a long time ago."

"What did he do?"

"He loved everybody."

"Us, too?"

"Yup."

"Why's the church all lit up, Keisha?
It's not Sunday."

"It's the night before Christmas, Tony.
Christmas isn't just Santa Claus. It's
Jesus' birthday and people come to
church to pray. See, in front of the
church—that's a statue of Jesus and
Mary, his mother."

"Like Mama and the baby!"

"Yup."

"Why's Jesus in that funny little house?"

"That's where Jesus was born. Weren't any hospitals then, like Mama went to when she had the baby."

"Why are all those animals in there?"

"It's a stable, where animals stay. That's the only place Joseph and Mary could find when it was time for Jesus to be born. Remember when we got evicted and Daddy couldn't find any place for us to stay?"

"Yup."

"What are those people singing about?"

"They're singing Christmas carols—
about Jesus."

"Can we sing, too?"

"You don't know the words."

"I'll just say,
*'Jesus, little baby Jesus,
like my baby brother.'* "

"Why are people putting money
in Santa Claus's basket?"

"They're giving money to poor people
who don't have anything."

"Can we put some money in his basket?"

"Mama gave us three dollars to spend.
You want to put one in the basket?"

"Yup."

"Why they have a star on top of
that tree?"

" 'Cause the shepherds taking care of
their sheep saw a real bright star over
the place where Jesus was born."

"Can we get a star for our tree?"

"It might cost too much.
We only have two dollars."

"Look, Keisha! The lady let me have it for just one dollar. It's the last one she had. We're lucky."

"Keisha, when Jesus was a baby,
did he have toys to play with?"

"He had presents, Tony."

"Three wise men were so glad he
was born, they traveled a long way
to bring him gifts."

"What did they give him?"

"One gave him gold—that's like money;
one gave him myrrh—like oil to rub on
his skin and make him feel good; and
one gave him frankincense to make him
smell good."

"The baby has oil to make him
feel good, and powder to make
him smell good, but he doesn't have
any money. We got one dollar
left. Can we give it to the baby?"

"Yup."

"Everybody's so friendly tonight,
Keisha, like they're happy."

"That's how Christmas makes you feel,
Tony."

"You know what I wish, Keisha?"

"What?"

"I wish Jesus had a birthday
every day—don't you?"

"Yup."